Patrick O'Brien

The Emerald Isle

A Poem

Patrick O'Brien

The Emerald Isle
A Poem

ISBN/EAN: 9783337408978

Printed in Europe, USA, Canada, Australia, Japan

Cover: Foto ©Andreas Hilbeck / pixelio.de

More available books at **www.hansebooks.com**

THE

EMERALD ISLE:

A Poem.

BY

REV. PATRICK O'BRIEN.

DEDICATED TO MY NATIVE LAND.

Erin, the beautiful Isle of my birth,
The dearest, sweetest spot on all the earth ;
Where'er I roam, though lovely lands I see,
My Irish heart still fondly turns to thee.

AUTHOR'S PREFACE.

"THE EMERALD ISLE" was suggested by Goldsmith's "Deserted Village," one of the sweetest poems in the English language. If the immortal Goldsmith had changed the title to the "Deserted Island," the description of scenery, the ruin and desolation portrayed in the "Deserted Village" would aptly apply to all Ireland. The author of "The Emerald Isle" began the poem with the intention of paraphrasing the "Deserted Village," applying its sentiments to Ireland; but when he finished the work, he found he had written an original poem, with the exception of a few descriptive passages (easily to be recognized by the reader), which are paraphrases of the latter poem. As it would be improper to use quotation marks in a paraphrase, the author here acknowledges his indebtedness to the great Irish poet, Goldsmith, for *every word* taken from his immortal works: "The Deserted Village" and "The Traveller." "The Emerald Isle" was written in 1874, immediately after the failure of Mr. Isaac Butt's Home Rule movement, and while the author was indignant at the insulting treatment accorded the Home Rule Bill and its advocates by the English members of Parliament. When "The

Emerald Isle" was composed, the author was strongly inclined to believe that Ireland would never gain her just rights by constitutional means. He was led to form this opinion by reason of the cruel injustice inflicted by England on Ireland for centuries, and on account of the savage manner in which Mr. Butt's Bill was cried down by the enemies of Ireland in Parliament. Since then, however, the new Irish Parliamentary party, led by Charles Stuart Parnell, has accomplished a wonderful work, and the author hopes that Ireland may yet gain her long-lost independence by constitutional agitation. May God grant she may never again be driven to resort to arms to compel England to give her back the rights so ruthlessly stolen centuries ago, and held to this day only by force of arms. It must be said to the credit of the Irish people that they never resorted to arms except in self-defence, and when goaded into rebellion by the tyrannical rule of a foreign government—the same government against which Americans rebelled over a hundred years ago, and after a long and bloody war of seven years, finally succeeded in gaining the independence which we now enjoy. Like the unconquerable Americans whom England tried to enslave by force of arms, the Irish people will never willingly submit to be enslaved by an alien power.   They have fought the Dane and the Saxon for nearly a thousand years, and though overpowered on the field of battle again and again by superior numbers and illimitable wealth, they have never been conquered.   A race that has fought for national liberty a thousand years is invincible.   They must eventually succeed in gaining their independence.   They must and shall be free to rule the country God gave them for their own use, and not the use of England.   The author offers this little poem as a Christmas gift to his native land.   The offering is small, but it comes from a heart upon which is indelibly stamped the beautiful image of his own loved " Emerald Isle."

PATRICK O'BRIEN.

CLEVELAND, OHIO, U.S. OF A.,   .
          Christmas, 1890.

· The · Emerald · Isle. · · ·

I.

Sweet Erin, loveliest Isle of all the seas,

Whose hills are fanned by many an od'rous breeze,

Whose shores are kissed around by ocean wave,

A blooming garden, but fair freedom's grave.

Land of my birth, I sing a song of thee,

Though far away, thou art still dear to me ;

Dear as when I trod thy carpet green,

And loved to dwell upon each lovely scene.

Oft I wandered on thy sea-girt shore,

And viewed thy sylvan charms o'er and o'er :

Oft I scanned the daisy-mantled plain,

And wondered when should end the tyrant's reign,

When the Flag of Green should proudly wave

Above the Isle of Saints and Emmet's grave,

When this charming paradise of earth

Should hail the glorious dawn of freedom's birth,

When her sons in one united host

Would rise in arms and cease the empty boast,

When the Saxon lord should flee her soil,

And leave it to her sturdy sons of toil :

To those whose fathers rightly owned the land,

From whom 'twas stolen with the sword in hand,

And held alone by force of armed might,

Without the shadow of a legal right.

Oft I wondered how these things could be,

When Erin's sons are panting to be free.

Where'er a child of Erin can be found,

He's ready for the fray at battle's sound ;

A million hands would grasp the trusty gun,

A million hearts would beat as only one.

Oh, for a leader in the battle's fray,

And Ireland's sons would surely gain the day.

We want a leader with a record true,

A well trained soldier, for none else will do ;

One who stood the test on gory field,

And ne'er to en'my made a cowardly yield ;

A man who loves the land for which he fights,

Who'll die for Irish homes and Irish rights ;

A man who hates the Saxon robber crew,

Who'll ne'er unto his country prove untrue ;

With judgment cool, and one who in defeat

Will stand again the hated foe to meet ;

One who, versed in all the science of war,

Can plan a battle and can see afar ;

One who'll follow up proud victory's path,

Or flee in order from the en'my's wrath.

If such a man to lead us can be found,

We'll meet the Saxon on our native ground,

We'll meet him as our fathers did of yore,

And fight the battle fought and lost before,

We'll meet him with the rifle in our hand,

And drive him from our own dear native land.

'Twas thus he first set foot upon our shore

And made our streams run red with Celtic gore ;

By force he conquered, and by force he reigns ;

By force we'll drive him from our fertile plains.

O'Connell tried the power of peaceful force,

(With what effect the reader knows, of course,)

The greatest master of the human mind

That we can boast, of our own race and kind,

The man who faced the lion in his den,

Supported by the voice of all true men ;

With peaceful weapons he did meet his foes,

And dealt them many hard and telling blows ;

With mind and heart he fought his country's fight,

And after years he gained one paltry right—

The right to sit and talk in London town,

Beneath the shadow of the royal crown ;

But words fall harmless on the tyrant's ears ;

He laughs at words,—-the sword alone he fears.

II.

But some will tell me, 'tis no use to fight ;

Though all agree 'tis not opposed to right.

" For seven weary centuries, or more,

"We've fought the Saxon tyrant o'er and o'er,

"We've fought and bled—alas! 'twas all in vain —

"It only served to draw more tight the chain ;

"Oh! foolish men, to tempt the battle o'er,

"When you were beat on many a field before ;

" 'Tis better far to bend beneath the yoke,

"Than spill one drop of blood by armèd stroke."

'Tis thus some patriots talk, who fear to fight,

And cower beneath the hand of armèd might ;

The glist'ning bay'net makes their blood run cold—

They're cowardly patriots, if the truth were told.

The British fought to gain our lovely land,

They entered Erin with the sword in hand.

Our fathers met them on the gory field,

O'erpowered by numbers they were forced to yield ;

But never, never did they cease the fight,

Though right was oft compelled to yield to might.

Our fathers ne'er surrendered with a will;

Shall we surrender now, or fight on still?

Shall we give up our land, our " Island Home,"

And, strangers through the world forever roam ?

Shall we abandon our beloved Isle,

And live and die in lonely, sad exile?

Shall we give up the land we've claimed so long,

The land of heroes, and the "Isle of Song?"

Give up those em'rald hills and flow'ry dells,

Where nature bright in all her beauty dwells?

No! no! now and forever, we shall cling

To the land that blossoms in perpetual spring—

To the land for which our sires have fought and bled,

Till the em'rald sward was changed to gory red.

No! we'll e'er defend her with our arms strong,

While Celtic blood shall course our veins along.

Though baffled oft, to England ne'er we'll yield,

We'll fight her still upon the bloody field.

III.

This language may appear to some too strong,

(I plead the license granted unto song),

I revel not in scenes of blood and fire ;

But how can I suppress my burning ire—

I, an Hibernian by birth and name,

Who glories in my darling country's fame,

Who loves his nation, and her foes despise,

Whose wrongs the scorching tear brings to his eyes,

The land in happy childhood oft I trod,

Where first I learned to know and love my God,

Where joy or sorrow hath endeared each scene

That blossoms fresh to-day, in mem'ry green.

Oh Erin! of all lands, by Heaven blest,

God grant my bones may in thy bosom rest.

Where'er I roam, though lovely lands I see,

My Irish heart still fondly turns to thee,

Where, 'round thy valleys gentle zephyrs stray,

And sylvan songsters pipe on every spray,

Where crystal streams their winding course pursue,

And daisies deck the meadows winter through,

Where all the seasons wear a temp'rate smile,

Throughout the varied year, in that blest Isle,

Where all creation's charms may be found,

Of mountain, river, lake and level ground,

There, Nature wears her choicest, loveliest dress,

And ever smiles in conscious loveliness.

Such is the charming Isle that gave me birth,

The dearest, sweetest spot on all the earth.

A land of plenty, and a land of slaves,

A land of tyrants, and proud, lordly knaves.

There, freedom cowers beneath the tyrant's frown,

And all must bend the knee to foreign crown.

Foreign lords possess the Irish soil,

Native slaves enrich them with their toil,

Foreign laws, the people bind in chains.

'Till scarce one trace of liberty remains ;

A few proud masters grasp the whole domain,

The fertile lands are now a grazing plain ;

The people fear the hungry lion's roar,

A wall of bay'nets stretches round her shore ;

Where once the happy peasant's cottage stood,

Is now a covert or a wild-fowl wood,

The smiling farm now forsaken lies—

Oh! sad, heart-rending scene to Irish eyes,

Where towns and happy hamlets once arose,

The favored cattle graze in quiet repose ;

The farmer's homestead leveled to the floor,

Himself is driven from his native shore,

Ne'er again, perhaps, to see his ruined home,

A stranger, round the world doomed to roam.

But I must cease to sing this mournful strain,

It breaks my aching heart, and gives me pain.

IV.

Awake! my harp, and wipe away the tear,

Let martial music greet my Celtic ear;

Let others sing the sad and mournful song,

Give me the strains that rouse the martial throng,

I have no tears to waste o'er Erin's plight,

Give me the rifle, and for her I'll fight.

Away with tears, and words, and childish fears,

They only rouse contempt, and mocking jeers

In those who rule my native land to-day—

Rule her, how? by hateful martial sway;

Words, prayers, and tears will never right her wrongs,

The sword alone can cut her galling thongs.

Froude himself hath said she should be free.

Thus far this man agrees with you and me;

But then, he says, she ne'er will see that day,

Unless she wins it in the battle's fray.

England ne'er will loose her iron hold,

No matter how the Irish talk and scold;

She fought and bled to win her Irish prey,

And she will fight to hold the land to-day,

She ne'er did grant a foot of soil in peace,

So talk no more, those cringing prayers cease.

Pray, tell me, where's the land her freedom won,

Without the use of arrow, sword or gun?

No, in all history there is not one.

The plucky Swiss can boast their William Tell.

Who for their freedom fought and nobly fell,

Columbia boasts her own great Washington,

Who fought the British and right nobly won:

Who hath not heard of Arnold Winkelreid,

Who broke the Austrian lines—his country freed,

If Ireland will be free, she too must fight,

'Tis thus those heroes gained their country's right.

All honor to that Continental band

Who freed Columbia from the tyrant's hand ;

All praise to Boston, where the English laws

Were first opposed in freedom's holy cause;

All praise to those, who, in that glorious day,

Poured England's tea into old Boston Bay.

Hurrah! for Valley Forge and Lexington,

Hurrah! hurrah! for our own Washington!

Oh! for a Washington for Ireland's cause,

Now groaning 'neath the hated British laws,

'Gainst which Columbia once in arms 'rose,

And drove beyond the sea her foreign foes.

V.

Fond mem'ry wafts me o'er the sea

To where my fathers sleep,

And the burning tear falls silently,

Though I would fain not weep.

Again I view each charming scene

Of happy childhood's time,

Again I gambol o'er the green,

In my own native clime.

The cottage where I once did dwell

I ne'er again shall see,

Beneath the tyrant's hand it fell,

How sad the thought to me.

The spreading tree, beneath whose shade,

I oft poured forth my lay,

No more it decks the lovely glade—

It, too, has passed away.

Dark desolation reigns supreme

Upon my native soil—

But I must drop this sad'ning theme,

It makes the hot blood boil.

VI.

Again my harp bursts forth in martial song,

As I sweep the trembling chords along ;

Whene'er I think of Ireland's wrongs, her woes,

I must sing vengeance on her hated foes.

Oh ! who can hear poor Erin's woeful tale,

The wrongs inflicted on the Irish Gael,

And still cry : " Peace, peace, my friends, be quiet!"

No ! no ! I say, go on, prepare to fight—

Fight till every English tyrant yields,

Fight for your homes, your children and your fields ;

The land is yours, 'tis held by force alone—

Fight, fight for that which is of right your own.

Weigh well the step you are about to take,

Rush in not madly, for your country's sake,

If you would be victorious in that day

Await your chance, and now prepare the way.

Such wild-goose chases as we've had before,

I hope and trust you'll ne'er repeat them o'er ;

They only serve to weaken Ireland's cause,

And forge anew the hateful curfew laws.

Work out your plans, and let them well mature,

Or else your movement never will endure.

All must unite in every land and clime,

All must be ready when shall come the time,

As all agree upon the end in view,

Let all the sure and only means pursue.

The signal gun must ring on Erin's shore,

And then her sons will quickly hasten o'er;

The men at home must prove they will be free,

Before we'll make a move beyond the sea.

Then talk no more of Home Rule or Repeal,

You now must know the only means is steel.

Your Representatives were flatly slapped,

And all the Tory side quite loudly clapped,

When, in the House was broached the Irish cause;

It fell 'mid thund'ring storms of applause.*

Those wordy patriots, who so loudly talk,

And round the Capitol so proudly stalk,

Had better lead their nation on the field,

And force the Briton *there* our rights to yield.

---

* Rejection of Isaac Butt's Home Rule Bill.

No true patriot but would gladly die,

If in rebellion Erin's flag should fly,

And he whose love of country then would cease,

Should not be honored in the time of peace,

The priest and layman would at once unite,

Whene'er the nation would rise up to fight;

Success is all we lack, to render just

The Irish cause.‡   *Unite*, succeed we must.

VII.

Oh! sons of Erin, now unite!

March on !   March on to battle !

Our cause is just, we have the right,

Then let the musket rattle.

---

‡ Or a reasonable hope of success.

Oh! let your banner proudly fly!

Ring loud the battle chorus:

We'll have our freedom, or we'll die,

We'll drive the foe before us.

Arise !   Arise ! for now's the time.

Oh !   don't let pass this hour !

March on !   March on ! from every clime,

In all your might and power.

Hurrah !   Hurrah ! for Erin's flag,

Ring out the battle chorus :

Pull down the tyrant's blood-stained rag,

We'll drive the foe before us.

VIII.

But soft, my harp, a milder strain pursue,

Those martial songs are ill becoming you,

The trembling hand that touches now thy chord

Is also consecrated to the Lord.

Now sing, my harp, of lovely, gentle peace,

And those wild songs of war and vengeance cease.

Sing now of Erin's fame in days of yore,

When peace and freedom reigned from shore to shore,

The Isle of learning and the Isle of rest,

A beacon bright that burned in the West,

When students filled her schools, before her fall,

And home and school were given free to all,

When Ireland, free from all outside restraints,

Did win the title of the "Isle of Saints,"

When Irish Monks went forth in Mission bands,

To Christianize the men of other lands,

When Brian's gentle scepter bore the sway,

And Erin saw her happiest, golden day.

IX.

Alas! this happy pleasing strain must cease,

And war again usurp the harp of peace.

The barbarous Dane set foot upon our shore,

And Erin's streams ran red with Celtic gore;

Two hundred years our fathers' blood they shed,

And all the joys of peace from Erin fled.

When Danish foes were driven from the land,

They were replaced by Saxons, sword in hand,

Celtic blood again in streams did flow,

Alas! in vain, for still remains the foe.

For seven hundred years a bloody strife

They waged against our luckless nation's life,

The Irish met them oft on many a field,

O'erpowered by numbers, they were forced to yield;

But never through those centuries of woe

Did Ireland cease to fight the foreign foe.

Suspended war again she will renew,

And every son of Erin, to his country true,

Will meet the Saxon, with his gun in hand,

And fight for freedom and his native land.

X.

Be not deceived, my friends, with doubtful hope,

Let not a faction with the en'my cope;

Let all your petty factious bands agree,

'Ere you attempt again your Isle to free:

Let curs'd dissension hence forever cease,

Among yourselves establish lasting peace.

Choose now your man to lead you on the way,

Let all, their leader, right or wrong, obey;

As long as he pursues the end in view,

He must be chief and be obeyed by you.

The greatest gen'ral may at times mistake,

But then his army should not him forsake;

The Great Napoleon did not always win,

And still his army ever clung to him.

Obedience is the first of martial laws,

The soldier ne'er must stop to doubt or pause.

An army is a body dumbly led,

The gen'ral in command the only head.

'Tis his alone to know the battle's plan,

And head the soldiers in the foremost van;

The private has no right to call to task

His leader, or him any questions ask.

Some chosen men should hold the pow'r supreme,

Remove, appoint, and act as they best deem;

They should be men of learning and of weight,

Well qualified to guide the ship of state.

Such men may now be found on Irish soil,

Who waste their time in legislative toil,

Proclaim in London their poor nation's ills,

And then go home with their rejected bills.

A VISION OF THE FUTURE.

XI.

Awake! my harp! cease this didactic strain,

And tune thy strings to martial song again:

Methinks I see the dawn of Freedom's day,

My blood grows warm for the coming fray;

Methinks I hear the tramp of armèd men,

Go marching home to fight the foe again.

Hark! the sound of war falls on my ear,

I see the bay'net bright and glist'ning spear;

There waves the Green and Gold, and there the Rec

There lie the groaning wounded, and the dead.

The smoking cannons roar, and sabres flash,

As on the Irish soldiers madly dash,

Hark! now I hear the Celtic battle cry—

ERIN-GO-BRAGH! rings out from earth to sky.

I look again! behold the British run—

The Green has conquered, and the field is won.

XII.

The sun has risen o'er my native Isle,

And now she wears sweet, gentle Freedom's smile,

The British flag no longer meets the eye,

The Flag of Green now proudly waves on high,

Old Erin is a nation once again,

The song of peace is heard in town and glen,

And Irish bards immortalize the dead

Who for their country nobly fought and bled.

Irish commerce dots the ocean wave,

A monument is raised o'er Emmet's grave,

A nation now we have, and call our own—

No more we bend the knee to foreign throne.

THE END.

www.ingramcontent.com/pod-product-compliance
Lightning Source LLC
Chambersburg PA
CBHW022207020726
47496CB00008B/2915